Tan's Fish

Illustrations by Theresa Sherman

LITT

Tan's Fish

by Ruthven Todd

An Atlantic Monthly Press Book

OWN AND COMPANY · Boston · Toronto

ATLANTIC-LITTLE, BROWN BOOKS
ARE PUBLISHED BY
LITTLE, BROWN AND COMPANY
IN ASSOCIATION WITH
THE ATLANTIC MONTHLY PRESS

*Published simultaneously in Canada
by Little, Brown & Company (Canada) Limited*

PRINTED IN THE UNITED STATES OF AMERICA

U. S. 1042988

For Nathan Wilbur

Tan's Fish

Canton

*I*N the city of Canton, capital of the prov-
ince of Kwangtung, in southern China, there lived
a boy called Tan. So far back as he could remember, which was quite a long way in his ten years,
Tan had loved to escape from the crowded, clut-
tered city into the countryside. The streets of the
city were narrow and crooked, but the rice fields
ran wide and open up to the mountains and the
tea plantations.

When Tan was seven, his father, a silk merchant, had given him four little aquariums. These had been set up in the courtyard of the house where he lived. Tan loved the little fish which darted this way and that like streaks not only of quicksilver but also, if there had been such stuff, quickgold.

Every year, whenever he was offered a present, he would ask either for more aquariums, or for some fish to put in those he already had. Sometimes he caught a few little wild fish himself, but the most exciting ones came from Mr. Won, the dealer in tropical fish.

Mr. Won was a good friend to Tan. Even when he knew that his little friend could not afford to buy any new fish, he allowed him to wander as he liked around the dim, mysterious shop, lit only by the wavery light that filtered through the water of the aquariums. There he gazed for as long as he wished into the tanks which held treasures from all the corners of the world.

In his room at home Tan had a big map of the world, and on this he would mark the places from which the different fish came. There were marks on Malaya, on Thailand, on Australia, on Africa, and even on far-off South America.

When he was grown up, Tan thought, he would lead an expedition to South America, to travel up the enormous river called the Amazon. In one of the little streams that ran into this river, he would find a fish that no one had ever seen before. It would be a fish so beautiful that everyone who saw it would exclaim with delight.

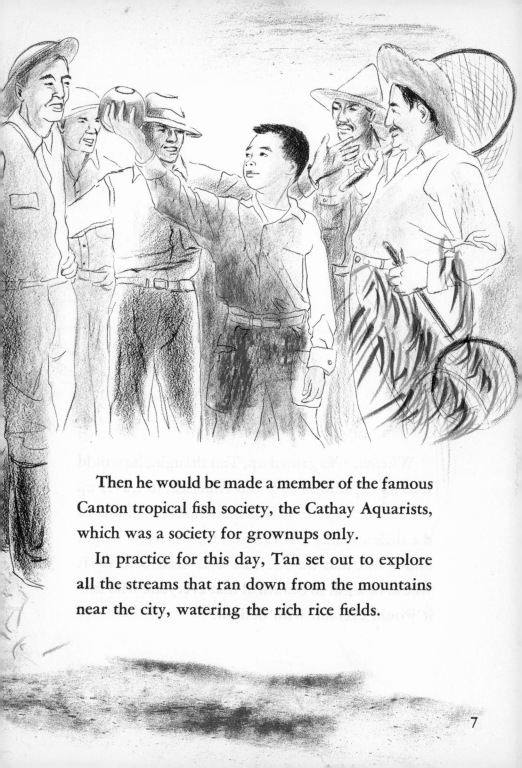

Then he would be made a member of the famous
Canton tropical fish society, the Cathay Aquarists,
which was a society for grownups only.

In practice for this day, Tan set out to explore
all the streams that ran down from the mountains
near the city, watering the rich rice fields.

His favorite streams were those that flowed down from the White Cloud Mountains, which rose into the air through wisps of cloud, some ten miles to the north of the city.

The trouble with these streams was that it took a long time to reach them. As Tan's mother and father wanted him to be home before dark, he usually had little time for exploration. Just as he thought he was getting somewhere, the lengthening shadows of the pines and wild cherries would remind him that it was time to start for home.

On a spring afternoon, after the snows had started to thaw, Tan found a stream he had not explored before. In order to water the rice fields that lay on each side of the stream, someone had made a dam out of great boulders and clay. Over the top of this the roiled water, brown with mud, was boiling furiously.

Perched on a dry corner of the dam, Tan looked down into the water below it, but it was far too thick for him to see anything as it swirled among

the rushes and flowering irises by the waterside.

Then, suddenly, in a momentary clearing of a corner of the pool, Tan thought he caught a glimpse of a little fish. Quickly the water was murky again. Still the flash that Tan's sharp eyes had caught was enough. He did not think he had ever seen a fish just like it before, either in Mr. Won's tanks or in his books with pictures of fish.

He could not try to
catch the fish, for now he
could not see anything.
Tan looked at the sun. It
was already down among
the topmost branches of
a tall, struggling pine,
showing it was time for
him to start back to the
city.

All the way home, Tan
kept telling himself that
on his next holiday, he
would surely see what the
little fish was really like,
and find out if it was one
he had in his tanks.

Time seemed to crawl
until his next holiday and
Tan had to go to school
and to help around the

house. Only once did he have a chance to visit Mr. Won's shop and look at the wonderful display of mysterious aquariums. He looked most carefully but was quite sure the little fish he had glimpsed was not there.

When, at long last, the day of the holiday finally

arrived, Tan was ready for it. He set out toward
the White Cloud Mountains, carrying a little net
and a globe with a string handle.

He started early in the day, for the journey was
a long one, and he wanted to have plenty of time
to spend beside his new stream.

As he made his way through the twisting streets
of the city, dodging the men carrying heavy
bundles on long poles and the handcarts piled high
with all kinds of merchandise, he tried to imagine
that he was an explorer setting out from one of the
cities of South America. He had heard there was a
pretty new fish to be found in a nearby stream. Of
course, hunting for tropical fish in South America
was really rather a dangerous job, for in all the
streams there were the dreaded piranhas. Although he had never seen a live one, Tan knew
about them and their needle-sharp teeth from Mr.
Won's books, and knew that they could tear a man
to pieces in a few minutes.

In a way Tan felt glad that he was not really

going to explore one of the tributaries of the Amazon but was only going to a stream near home, where the worst that was likely to happen was that he would find a fat black leech clinging to his bare leg. In a pocket he carried a little jar of salt, just in case this happened. A good explorer was prepared for anything, and salt sprinkled on a leech would make it let go.

Tan had not got far out of the city before an old farmer, seated on a wide, horned water buffalo, ambled up beside him.

"Jump up behind," said the old man. "We both seem to be going the same way."

Tan thought how nice a ride would be, as he would not be at all tired when he reached his stream. He scrambled up on the back of the water buffalo, behind the farmer, clutching his globe and net. The slow beast plodded on along the road, which ran between well-watered fields of rice, clumps of rushes and bamboo marking the courses of the ditches.

"Where are you bound for, boy?" asked the old farmer, turning his head to look curiously at the globe and net.

"I'm going to the White Cloud Mountains to catch a fish," said Tan.

"There won't be much eating on all the fish you'll catch with that little net or carry in that little globe," said the farmer, laughing.

Tan laughed too.

Then he tried to explain that he did not want the fish as food, but only for his collection of live fish. He said it was a special kind of little fish, one that he had never seen before, and he wanted it to keep in an aquarium.

But the old farmer could think of fish only as part of a meal. He could not understand how anyone would want to *look* at a live fish or keep it as a pet.

Tan was grateful for the ride, which took him nearly to the place where he would have to leave the road to find his stream again.

This time the water was as clear as the glass of the globe Tan carried. He went up the hill beside the stream toward the dam. There were flowering rushes and irises by the water, and on either side lay the rice fields which were irrigated by the dam. A few butterflies danced in the bright spring air. Up beyond rose the White Cloud Mountains, their peaks feathery with white clouds.

Slowly and cautiously Tan drew near the water below the dam. Lying flat on his stomach, he looked down into the shallow crystal pool.

He could hardly prevent himself from shouting aloud with joy and excitement.

Down there in the clear water were many silvery little fish with bright white stripes along their sides, and gay fins of different colors.

He had been right. He had never seen these fish before.

Ever so gently, he lowered his net into the water. The little fish scurried away in fright. Tan did not chase them with his net, but just lay there perfectly still. After a short while the little fish grew used to the net lying on the bottom. They darted all around and over it.

Tan held his breath and waited until a particularly gaily colored fish was right over the mouth of the net.

Then, with a quick flick of his wrist, he raised the net above the surface, while the other fish flashed madly away.

Tan lowered his globe into the cool mountain water and filled it. Then he tilted the new fish into its carrier.

There, swimming round and round the little glass globe, was the most beautiful fish that he had ever seen. There were blue and yellow in the fin along the back and orange in the tail, while the white stripe glowed like moonstone.

Again and again that day Tan lowered his net into the water and waited without moving. Each time he came up with another little fish.

After he had nine or ten of the new fish in the globe, he decided that he had enough of them for the tank which, in high hopes, he had prepared for them at home. Then, carefully, for the little fish were rather crowded in the globe, he started slowly back toward the city.

Once back on the road, he went so cautiously that several people on water buffaloes caught up with him and offered him a ride atop the bundles the buffaloes carried behind the riders. These kindly passers-by would cry, "Ho, boy, what have you got there? Jump up behind!"

But Tan answered each of them politely, saying, "Thank you very much, sir, but I'd rather walk. I don't want to risk spilling my fish."

And so he went on his way, slowly and carefully.

It was nearly dusk when he got back to the winding streets of Canton, which were still as crowded and busy as ever. He wanted to start running, for he was eager to show off his new finds to his friends. But he was too afraid of slopping the water out of the globe and losing his fish.

At last, however, he reached home. He went to the tanks in the courtyard. He put his finger in the water of the new tank which he had made ready. The temperature seemed to be much the same as that of the water in the globe.

Gently, Tan lowered his globe into the tank and tilted it so that the fish could swim out. When there were only two left, he took the globe out of the aquarium again.

Still carrying his prize with the greatest of care, he went through the narrow streets until he reached the shop of his friend Mr. Won.

Mr. Won was busy with a customer when Tan came into the shop, but he turned to see what the boy was carrying.

"What have you got there, Tan?" he asked curiously.

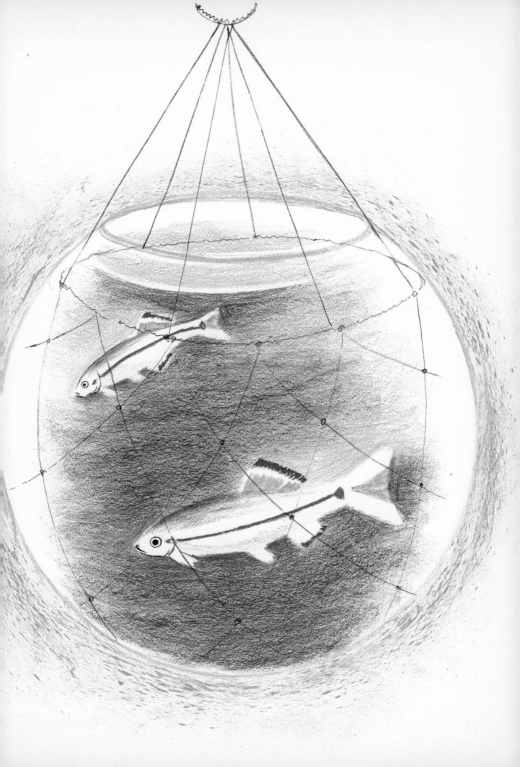

Tan tried to hide his excitement, but his voice trembled just a little.

"Nothing much," he said as carelessly as he could. "Just a pair of little fish."

Then it was too much for him and he blurted out, "I don't think you've ever had any just like them!"

"Nonsense," replied Mr. Won, but his voice was kindly. He was terribly proud of the fact that he had the best selection of tropical fish in the whole of the great city of Canton.

He came forward and peered, through thick glasses, into Tan's globe.

He sucked in his breath, wagging his mustache as he did so, and looked even more closely.

Then he spoke slowly. "I wouldn't know for certain, Tan, but I think you may have something new here."

He turned to the tall, thin customer who was watching a Siamese fighting fish huffing and puffing at itself in a little bit of a mirror.

"Dr. Lin," he said, "would you come over here and take a look?"

The man whom Tan had thought a customer came forward, and Mr. Won said, "This is Dr. Lin, the head of the Fisheries Experiment Station. Dr. Lin, I should like you to meet my friend Tan."

The tall stranger took Tan's hand and shook it. He glanced carelessly down into the globe and then he, too, took a long second look.

"This fish is new to me, Mr. Won," he said finally, and his voice showed his excitement. "I've never seen it before, myself." Then he seemed to remember that he was an expert, and he went on more slowly, "Of course, I'll have to check and see. I wonder, Mr. Tan, if you could possibly let me have a couple of your fish? If you can, I should then be able to identify them for certain."

Tan, who might have been unwilling to part with his new finds so soon, was greatly impressed that no less a person than the head of the Fisheries Experiment Station was interested in his fish.

After a moment's thought, during which he decided that as he was the explorer who had done the finding, the rest was up to the stay-at-home scientists, he said politely, "If Mr. Won will lend me a globe, I'll go home and get another pair for Dr. Lin."

He put down his own globe and, with Mr. Won's globe clutched firmly to him, ran off through the crowded streets toward his home.

When Tan arrived, panting, in the courtyard, his father, who was gazing at the blossoms on a peach tree, looked round at him curiously.

"What are you up to in such a hurry?" he asked.

Tan told him that he had found a new fish. His father smiled, but when he heard that Dr. Lin of the Fisheries Experiment Station was interested in it, he became serious.

He held the globe for Tan while he scooped up another couple with a little net.

"I hope you are right," Tan's father said, "and that they really are new. They are certainly very beautiful."

Walking carefully, Tan again set off for Mr. Won's shop.

When he arrived at the shop this time, it was filled with men. Two members of the Cathay Aquarists had come into the shop and had found Dr. Lin and Mr. Won stooped over Tan's globe, talking excitedly.

The two fish fanciers had taken a look for themselves and had then sent messengers for their friends. Now they were all trying to buy the fish from Mr. Won.

"But they are not mine to sell," Mr. Won was saying. "They belong to my friend Tan. Ah, here he is now."

The members of the society crowded round Tan, who was holding Mr. Won's globe.

"I will give you so much for your fish," cried one.

"Pooh," said another, "I'll give you three times that!"

"What are you trying to do" asked a third, "cheat the boy? I'll double that offer!"

"The fish are not for sale. I brought them for Mr. Won, for himself," Tan said, handing the globe to Dr. Lin, who took it as if it might shatter at his touch.

The members of the Cathay Aquarists looked terribly downcast.

Tan thought it might be nice to cheer them up.

"No," he said, "these fish are not for sale, but I'll tell you where you can get some for yourselves."

Then the men seemed to go crazy with excitement.

Mr. Won closed his shop, and the crowd, with Dr. Lin carrying his globe, accompanied Tan to his home. In a city of many processions, one more

or less did not seem to worry the passers-by who jumped out of the way of the chattering throng.

Tan's father was still in his twilit courtyard, but this time, instead of examining peach blossoms, he was looking down into the tank which held his son's new fish.

He shook hands with everyone and then they all started speaking at the same time. They were trying to persuade Tan's father that his son should be allowed to take the next day off from school.

"Well," he said slowly, "I don't know about that." But Tan saw the smile in his eyes and knew he was going to be given the extra holiday.

"It's really quite important," said Dr. Lin.

Tan's father smiled with his mouth.

"Just for once," he said, "I don't suppose it will do much harm, but it mustn't become a habit."

"I don't expect to find a new fish very often," said Tan solemnly, and everyone laughed.

Then Dr. Lin went away, carrying the globe.

He was Tan's first visitor in the morning, and

though he looked a little tired, his thin face was
bright with a smile.

"They're new fish, all right, Mr. Tan. I sat
up most of the night trying to find if they'd been
reported before. There are several rather like
them, but there's no doubt these are new."

Tan was terribly pleased. In all his dreams of
finding a new fish he had always been in some
strange place, such as the Congo basin, or a river
in South America. Now he had done exactly what
famous fish hunters did, but near his own home.
He was already a fully fledged fish explorer.

Soon after this, an enormous old car, looking far

too big for the narrow streets, drew up beside the house. The battered canvas top had given way years before, and it was so crowded with members of the Cathay Aquarists, loaded down with huge metal tanks and nets, that it looked as though there would hardly be room for Tan.

Finally, by squeezing a very fat fish fancier until it seemed he would burst, they made a space for the most important member of the expedition.

Then the car, with much grumbling at the load

it was carrying, started off, the driver hooting the horn to clear a path for it through the narrow streets. Tan's father and mother watched them until they were out of sight.

Owing to the roughness of the road, the car could not go nearly as far toward the mountains as the water buffalo had gone with Tan and the old farmer the day before.

They had to get out and walk along the edges of the fields which were watered by the streams which flowed down, cool and crystal, from the White Cloud Mountains.

The fattest fish fancier made hard going of it, puffing along gallantly behind all the others. Every time they came to a stream, he would look hopefully at Tan, gasping, "Is this it, boy?"

Tan had to shake his head, as he was afraid of laughing, and again the fat man snorted along behind them. When, at last, they came in sight of the dam, he was panting so loudly that it almost seemed he might frighten the fish with his noise.

The members of the society crept forward and peered at the shallow pool.

Sure enough, there were
hundreds of the little fish
swimming around, spark-
ling like sudden splashes
of quicksilver in the cold,
clear water.

The nets the men used
were bigger than Tan's
own, though the mesh was
just as small, and they
went about their fishing
in a different way. They
surrounded the pool and
all waded into it together,
so that the fish were scared
into swimming toward the
center.

Tan was more than a
little worried by the number of fish which the men
were catching. It seemed

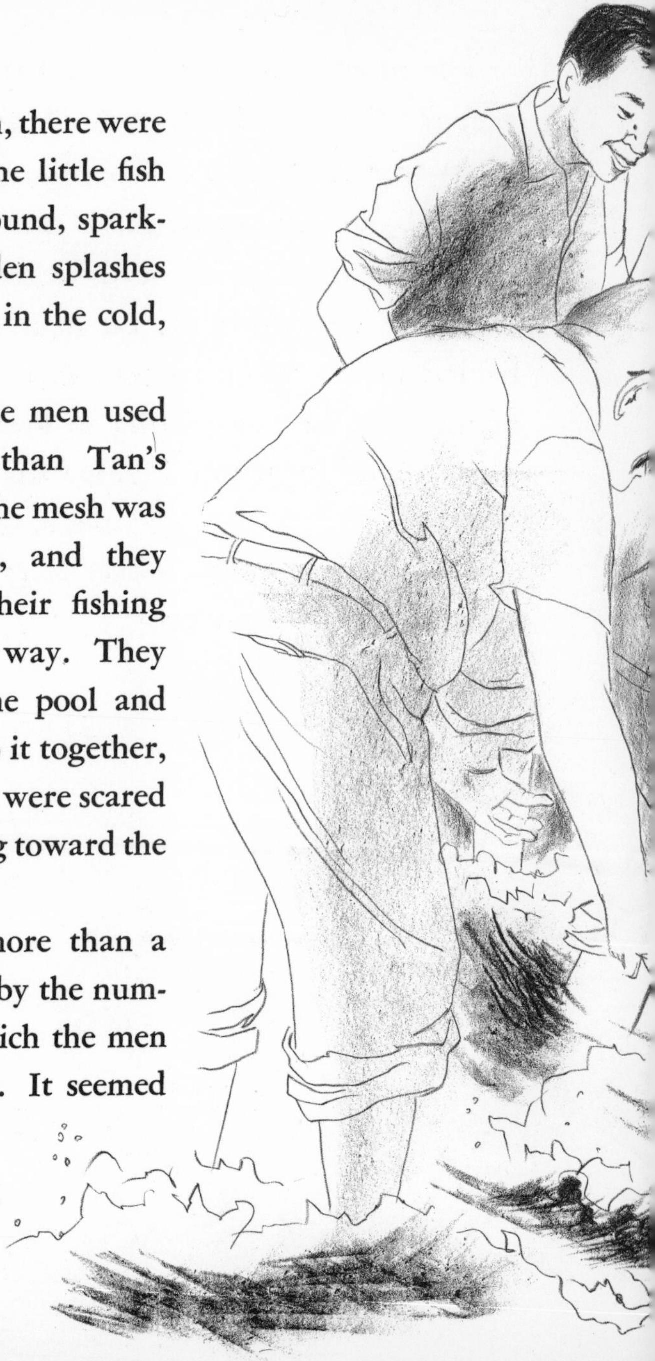

to him they caught so many that there soon would be none left in the pool, and still they went on fishing. But he did not like to say anything, for he supposed the members of the Cathay Aquarists knew more than he did.

When, at last, it seemed that if there were any fish left, they must be hiding under pebbles, the men started off over the fields once more.

Now they went more slowly, for the metal tanks

were full of water and were terribly heavy. Even the fattest fish fancier was able to roll along at a pace which suited him.

On the journey back to Canton the members of the society all said how grateful they were to Tan. He noticed that the driver of the old car, in between hooting the horn, was deep in conversation with a dignified white-bearded old man who sat beside him on the front seat. This old man was the president of the Cathay Aquarists.

When the car, after jostling its way through the clatter and clutter of the streets, drew up at Tan's house, he got out and was just about to run in and tell his parents about his day when the president stopped him.

"Although the rules of our society do not allow the admission of any member under the age of twenty," he said, "we have decided to make a special exception in your case. You are now a member of the Cathay Aquarists."

The members clapped and Tan said that he felt

honored indeed. Inside himself, however, he was still worried by the number of fish they had carried away from the stream.

He could not help it, but by this time he had started thinking of the little fish as *his* fish, and he noticed that his fellow members of the Cathay Aquarists also called it "Tan's Fish."

At home, before going to school in the morning and after coming home in the afternoon, he watched the fish in his own tank. He was not only

surprised but also delighted when, one afternoon, he discovered a few tiny eggs floating about.

He moved these eggs into another tank, in case the grown-up fish ate them. A few days later he was overjoyed when, looking into the spare tank, he saw there were about twenty tiny fish swimming around.

He went to see his friend Mr. Won, carrying a few of the baby fish as a gift, and with Mr. Won he showed them to the other members of the Cathay

Aquarists. They, too, soon found that the little fish had accepted captivity happily and had started to breed in their tanks.

One day, the day before a holiday, Tan received a notice from the Cathay Aquarists. It said there was to be an extraordinary, most important meeting on the following evening and that his attendance was particularly requested. Tan wondered what this could be about, and showed the notice to his father, who shook his head in surprise.

"Maybe," he suggested, "they are going to show yet another new fish."

That might well be so, for Mr. Won was always getting new shipments in from all over the world. Still, Tan thought, they would never show him any fish that he liked as well as he did *his* fish, the fish that *he* had found.

The holiday was a fine day and so Tan went out of the city. He knew where he was going. He was going back to the stream where he had found *his* fish.

The irises were now podded, and the blades of the rushes and bamboos were broader and tougher as he pushed his way through them to look into the sparklingly clear water, but, when he came to the dam, look as he might, Tan could seen none of the glittering little fish which had so delighted him before.

He went up and down the stream, peering anxiously into every pool. After searching all day, he had seen only two fish.

Late that afternoon he was back among the narrow winding streets of Canton, caring nothing for the jostling and buffeting he took from the hurrying crowds. He felt terribly sad. He had been careful himself not to take too many fish, but *his* fish had proved to be too popular with the Cathay Aquarists. It was clear now that they had not thought what they were doing.

It was with a heavy heart indeed that Tan went to the meeting that evening.

When he entered the big room with all the tanks around the walls, he could hardly bear to look at the shining, darting bodies of *his* fish.

All the members clapped when he came in and he was more than a little surprised, but still he was not cheered.

Suddenly Dr. Lin appeared on a platform at one end of the hall. In his hand he carried a bundle of papers. He started to read and Tan tried to pay attention, but his mind was too filled with sorrowful thoughts of the emptied stream. He was sure that none of the professional explorers would ever have left any of the streams that flowed into the Amazon or the Congo without its fair share of fish. A good fish explorer would *never* do that.

Then Tan heard his own name mentioned and, forgetting his sadness for a moment, he listened.

"And so," announced Dr. Lin, "in honor of the discoverer of this new fish I have given it the scientific name of *Tanichthys albonubes* — Tan's White Cloud Fish!"

魚 雲 白 的 唐

Then there was tremendous cheering and clapping and Tan looked around him in bewilderment. They were calling upon him to make a speech.

He had never made a speech before and there were so many people there. His knees knocked together as he stood up and looked at them all.

He bowed politely to Dr. Lin and then to his fellow members of the Cathay Aquarists.

"It is very nice of you to call the little fish after me," he said slowly, "and I am honored indeed. But today I am also unhappy." He paused and the people around him looked puzzled.

"Today," Tan went on, "I went back to the stream where I first found my fish. Today I found that there were none of them left, or only a very few. We have taken too many of them out of the stream. All I myself can do to help right this is to empty the fish out of my own tanks, where they

have bred, and pour them back into the stream. In this way I can perhaps help to restock it."

He was interrupted by the cries of his fellow members. They were all looking rather ashamed of themselves.

"There's no need for you to do that! I'll give six dozen!"

"I'll give five dozen!"

"I've done well and I'll give two hundred!"

They crowded round Tan and it was arranged that, early the next day, they would take the great old car and go round to the members collecting fish in order to return them to the stream.

As the meeting finally broke up, Dr. Lin came up to Tan.

"I will walk home with you," he said, and they set out through the twisting streets. On the way they talked of many things, including Tan's dreams of becoming an explorer. Tan found that Dr. Lin understood his dreams.

When they reached Tan's house, they found his father waiting for them. Tan told him his news about the fish's name and Dr. Lin consented to come in and have some of the special tea that Tan's father kept for distinguished visitors and old friends. This was taken from tiny, handleless cups, ages old, and poured from a beautiful porcelain pot.

"Do you think I could have another day off from school?" Tan asked at last.

His father shook his head. "I said it was just for once."

Dr. Lin explained about Tan's unhappiness at the way in which the stream had been emptied of his fish. He was very persuasive. In the end, Tan's father gave way. The head of the Canton Fisheries Experiment Station was an important man, and Tan's father knew that when he said it was important to his son, he meant that it really was important.

Tan dreamed of strange streams and even stranger fish all night, and in the morning, went out to his tanks. He carefully selected three dozen of the finest fish, and when the big car drew up, honking, outside, he emptied them into one of the large metal tanks on top of which smiling men were perched.

Everyone seemed happy on that journey and, going slowly across the fields toward the dam, even the fattest fish fancier seemed to make good and cheerful time.

When, at last, they reached the pool, the first of the tanks was tipped into the bright clear water.

As the sparks of silver glinted in the sunlight, Tan stood and was glad that, after all, he had not been responsible for taking the White Cloud Mountain fish away from their stream for good.

He looked at all *his* little fish, which had been born in aquariums, swimming about in a much bigger world than they had ever known, and his heart was happy.

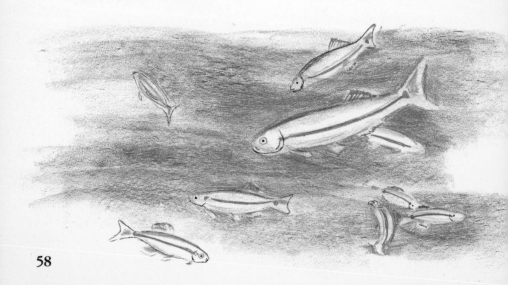